It may look like four against one, but Luna Girl is never alone. While she tries to spread airborne mischief with her winged minions, fly to the rescue and find these fluttering butterflies:

Three heads are better than one—and six heads are better than three! Romeo uses his Multiplying Machine to build an army of villains. Can you find them all?

Romeo is never too busy to cook up trouble! Look for these objects he might use in his next cunning plot:

Owlette's Owl Glider soars through the sky, just like she does! So, when a villain like Night Ninja tries to reach new heights, Owlette rises to the challenge. Capture these flags that Night Ninja has planted up high:

Even mad scientists don't always get it right the first time. Find these inventions that need some fixing up before Romeo uses them:

The Wolfy Kids are making trouble again, and it's up to the PJ Masks to stop them! Help the heroes find these signs of the Wolfy Kids' mischief:

In the nighttime, the PJ Masks battle baddies in their super-cars. But in the daytime, Connor, Amaya, and Greg zip and zoom on their super-cool bikes. Look around for these other sunny playthings:

Night Ninja is trying to cover the museum with a sticky layer of splats! Head back and help the PJ Masks clean up by finding sticky splats in these colors:

red
orange
yellow
green
blue
purple

Flutter back to the butterflies and find these characters:

one who has wings (but isn't an insect)
one who can climb up walls
one who uses a Luna Magnet
one who was built by a baddie
one who has super hearing

March back to the Multiplying Machine and count:

1 mad scientist
2 Luna Boards
3 heroes
4 moths
5 sticky splats

Romeo is trouble, and trouble starts with t. Race back to Romeo's lab and find these items that start with t, too:

toy truck
trophy
tires
tennis ball
toolbox
tree

Fly back to the Owl Glider and use your owl eyes to spot these patterns:

Go back and tinker with Romeo's inventions while you look for ordinary things that are:

behind Gekko
under Catboy
next to Romeo
between Owlette and a smiley friend
in front of Romeo's Robot

The Wolfy Kids sure have made a mess! Run back to the bones and find **20** Wolfy paw prints.

When they're not in uniform, the PJ Masks use their bikes to get around. Ovals and circles and spheres are all *around* too! Go back to the playground and find these round things:

Uh-oh! Night Ninja sent a teeny-weeny Ninjalino to spy on the PJ Masks! Go back through the book and find him hidden in every scene.